Dear Parents:

Congratulations! Your child is taking the first steps on an exciting journey. The destination? Independent reading!

STEP INTO READING® will help your child get there. The program offers five steps to reading success. Each step includes fun stories and colorful art or photographs. In addition to original fiction and books with favorite characters, there are Step into Reading Non-Fiction Readers, Phonics Readers and Boxed Sets, Sticker Readers, and Comic Readers—a complete literacy program with something to interest every child.

Learning to Read, Step by Step!

Ready to Read   Preschool–Kindergarten
• big type and easy words • rhyme and rhythm • picture clues
For children who know the alphabet and are eager to begin reading.

Reading with Help   Preschool–Grade 1
• basic vocabulary • short sentences • simple stories
For children who recognize familiar words and sound out new words with help.

Reading on Your Own   Grades 1–3
• engaging characters • easy-to-follow plots • popular topics
For children who are ready to read on their own.

Reading Paragraphs   Grades 2–3
• challenging vocabulary • short paragraphs • exciting stories
For newly independent readers who read simple sentences with confidence.

Ready for Chapters   Grades 2–4
• chapters • longer paragraphs • full-color art
For children who want to take the plunge into chapter books but still like colorful pictures.

STEP INTO READING® is designed to give every child a successful reading experience. The grade levels are only guides; children will progress through the steps at their own speed, developing confidence in their reading. The F&P Text Level on the back cover serves as another tool to help you choose the right book for your child.

Remember, a lifetime love of reading starts

Step into Reading, Random House, and the Random House colophon are registered trademarks
of Penguin Random House LLC.

Visit us on the Web!
StepIntoReading.com
randomhousekids.com

Educators and librarians, for a variety of teaching tools, visit us at
RHTeachersLibrarians.com

Library of Congress Cataloging-in-Publication Data
Names: Depken, Kristen L., author. | DiCicco, Sue, illustrator.
Title: The little red caboose : adapted from the beloved Little Golden Book written by
Marian Potter and illustrated by Tibor Gergely / by Kristen L. Depken ; illustrated by Sue DiCicco.
Description: New York : Random House, [2018] | Series: Step into reading.
Step 1, ready to read | Summary: A little red caboose thinks nobody cares for him
until he prevents his train from slipping backwards down a mountain.
Identifiers: LCCN 2016050008 | ISBN 978-1-5247-1426-0 (trade)
| ISBN 978-1-5247-1427-7 (glb) | ISBN 978-1-5247-1428-4 (ebook)
Subjects: | CYAC: Railroad trains—Fiction.
Classification: LCC PZ7.D4396 Lit 2018 | DDC [E]—dc23
LC record available at https://lccn.loc.gov/2016050008

Printed in the United States of America
10 9 8 7 6 5 4 3 2 1

This book has been officially leveled by using the F&P Text Level Gradient ™ Leveling System.

STEP INTO READING®

STEP 1 READY TO READ

THE LITTLE RED
Caboose

Adapted from the beloved Little Golden Book
written by Marion Potter and illustrated by Tibor Gergely

by Kristen L. Depken
illustrated by Sue DiCicco

Random House 🏠 New York

4

The little red caboose
is always last.

The big black engine

is always first.

Puff, puff.

Chuff, chuff.

The boxcars
are next.

Then the oil cars.

Then the coal cars.

Then the flat cars.

Then the little red
caboose.

Boys and girls wave
at the big black engine.

They listen
to all the cars
go <u>clickety-clack.</u>

But they do not
stay and listen
to the little red caboose.
He always comes last.

"Oh, smoke!"
says the little
red caboose.

He does not want
to come last.

The train starts
up a long, tall mountain.

Up goes
the big black engine.

Up go the boxcars.
Up go the oil cars,
the coal cars,
and the flat cars.

The little red caboose
is last.

Uh-oh!
The train is
slowing down.

It cannot get
up the mountain!

The train starts
to slip backward.

Look out,
little caboose!

The little red caboose
slams on his brakes.
He holds the train
to the tracks.

He saves the train
from sliding
down the mountain!

27

Bump!

Two black engines come.
They push the train
up to the top
of the mountain.

Everyone cheers.
The boys and girls wave
at the big black engines.

"We could not have
done it without
the little red caboose,"
they say.

Now everyone waves
at the little red caboose,
who saved the train!